THE LOST DIARY OF
TUTANKHAMUN'S MUMMY

Other Lost Diaries recently discovered
The Lost Diary of King Henry VIII's Executioner
The Lost Diary of Erik Bloodaxe, Viking Warrior
The Lost Diary of Julius Caesar's Slave

The Lost Diary of Tutankhamun's Mummy

Dug up by Clive Dickinson

Collins

An imprint of HarperCollins*Publishers*

First published in Great Britain by Collins in 1997

3 5 7 9 1 0 8 6 4

Collins is an imprint of HarperCollins*Publishers* Ltd,
77 - 85 Fulham Palace Road, Hammersmith, London W6 8JB

Text © Clive Dickinson 1997
Illustrations © George Hollingworth 1997
Cover illustrations © Martin Chatterton 1997
ISBN 000 694579 1

Printed and bound in Great Britain by
Caledonian International Book Manufacturing Ltd,
Glasgow, G64

MESSAGE TO READERS

In January 1878 a tall block of carved stone weighing 186 tons and standing nearly twenty metres tall arrived in wet, cold London. For over 3000 years this obelisk had been standing and then lying in the much nicer climate of Egypt. Originally it had been planned to put Cleopatra's Needle, as the obelisk became known, in front of the Houses of Parliament. When it turned out to be too heavy to go there it was erected beside the River Thames, where it can still be seen today.

Workmen putting the obelisk on the Embankment, found what looked like a battered old mat stuck to the bottom. During a lunch-break they pulled this off and found it was actually a bundle of papyrus paper covered in ancient Egyptian writing and pictures.

One of the men who found it decided it would make a useful mat for his lunch and for over a hundred years it lay in his lunchbox. This same lunchbox eventually turned up in a junk shop and was bought by Clive Dickinson, when digging around for a bargain. When he opened the lunch box, the ancient papers were found again.

Careful study by the Egyptian experts Dr Sandy Slippers and Dr Haventa Klue revealed that what the Victorian workman had used to lay his lunch on was in fact the work of one of the most amazing people living in the ancient times. She was a queen and seemed to have been mother of the best known Egyptian king - Tutankhamun. The bundle of papers was nothing less than the lost holiday diary of Nefertidy, Tutankhamun's mummy. Inside the diary were several postcards, apparently never sent. Extracts from the diary and the postcards that remained intact are published here for the very first time. They give a unique view of life in Ancient Egypt through Nefertidy's eyes as she cruised down the river Nile.

THEBES

Well, you could have knocked me down with the most expensive ostrich feather in Thebes when my dear boy told me his surprise! I know he's the Pharaoh and can do whatever he wants, even though he's only nine years old, but even I wasn't expecting this.

I knew he was up to something. I'd seen him whispering to his little friend Ankhy Pankhy and sneaking glances at me, thinking I hadn't noticed. I overheard words like 'out of the way for a long time', and 'get lost for ever', so I knew he was up to something extra special. And then he told me.

'Mum, you know you're always telling me how important the River Nile is to everyone in Egypt. Well, I was wondering how you'd like a bit of a break – a nice long break – like a cruise all the way down the river to Giza, to see the pyramids.'

To be honest, I've never been very interested in the pyramids. Who wants to wander round boring old piles of stones that have been collecting dust for over 1200 years? That's what tourists do, as I told Tutti.

'Yes, but tourists don't travel in the royal barge, stopping to stay with their friends and shopping at places like Herrods with other people's money, do they?'

I had to admit that he was right and the more I thought about it, the more I liked the idea of cruising in luxury, being pampered and having everything paid for with everyone looking *up* to me for a change. I also fancied visiting my childhood friend Nicencleen who lives out at the Faiyum and I could spend a few days in Memphis with Helvis and Preslettiti and shop till I drop with exhaustion.

That's why I started writing you, dear diary.
I know I get a bit forgetful and muddled and I
thought this would help me remember all the
lovely things I'm going to see and do while
I'm away. I thought it would be a nice present
for Tutti when I get back – whenever that is.

Now, I must go for my bath. . . or is it my
wig fitting. . . or my new robe. . . or my
lunch? If only someone would invent
something clever that reminds you of all the
things you have to do without you having to
remember them, but I suppose that's like
imagining you could fly through the air from
here to Giza instead of going by river.

We do have funny ideas don't we?

FIVE THINGS
TO DO BEFORE I GO

1. Get a map.

Mediterranean Sea

Giza

Heliopolis

Memphis

Faiyum

Akhenaten

Abydos

Valley of Kings

Thebes

Tutti gets so cross with me when I get things wrong, especially when I get lost or go the wrong way. So I'm going to get really organized for this lovely holiday. One of the nice priests called Twink Eltwinkel is helping me. He is very good at finding his way about. He knows how to use the stars to find where the north is. Apparently that's terribly important. Once you know where north is you can work out where everywhere else is. At least I think that's what he told me. Anyway I am travelling north on my holiday and he gave me a map which is awfully useful because he says it will show me where I'm going and where I am when I'm there.

I suppose that makes sense.

2. Pray to Hapy.

Hapy, as I learnt when I was a very little girl, is the god of the River Nile. So I must remember to say a few prayers to him if I want to enjoy my holiday. I don't want the river to leave me high and dry on a mudbank. Neither do I

want an enormous flood that would sweep me right down to the Mediterranean Sea.

Of course Hapy gets quite a lot of prayers because without HIM we'd all be in the black and sticky, as Tutti would say. Actually that's not quite right, because it's Hapy who brings *wonderful* black mud down the river every year when the Nile floods. That's why we call the soil beside the river 'black earth'. I've heard that other people don't think much of having their fields covered with black mud, but we ancient Egyptians (and the young ones too) love it because it makes our crops grow marvellously. When the crops grow well there's a good harvest, with plenty to eat and everyone's happy with Hapy.

I may not be the greatest geographer in Egypt but I do know the difference between the Black Land and the Red Land. Naturally, I wouldn't dream of going into the Red Land myself. It's a terrible place – wild and empty with only sand and dust and rocks as far as you can see. There's not a drop of water, so I can only imagine what the people there must smell like if they can't wash! And, as any Egyptian will tell you, smelling nasty is very sinful. The gods don't like it and neither do I.

3. Decide when to come back.

Time is something that Tutti and I don't always agree on. He says I have no idea about time. Listening to him you'd think the most embarrassing thing for a pharaoh is to have a mother who is always in the wrong place at the wrong time. Is that why he's sending me on this holiday? Well I shall let him know exactly when I am coming back and I shall stick to it, whatever happens. One thing I'm sure about is that I must be back by New Year. Well, no one in Egypt would want to miss New Year unless they were really stupid – or lived right out in the middle of the dreadful Red Land.

My friend the god Hapy makes sure that New Year always comes at the beginning of summer. He sends a special sign, just in case people like me get a bit confused. At New Year Hapy makes the water in the river start to rise. As the water gets higher that's when the river floods all the fields bringing that nice thick black, squidgy, sludgy mud that everyone has been waiting for. So, I must be back for the New Year Celebrations to have that very special mud facepack and to sing *Old Long Nile* with all my friends. I'm not sure that Tutti will think it's a long enough holiday though. It'll only be about forty days and forty nights and the dear sweet boy wants me to have a *really* long holiday. He said something about being off my trolley, some kind of slang for needing a rest, I dare say.

4. Say goodbye to my old friends.

While the servants are finishing my packing and getting everything ready on the royal barge, I thought I would just pop over the river to the other side to say goodbye to a few old 'friends'. They're not friends in the way that my friends in Thebes are friends. These ones are rather special. For one thing most of them are kings. They're also very old. And they're buried underground because they've all gone to their afterlife in the Underworld.

The place where I go and visit them is called the Valley of the Kings. Only the very top people get buried there. Tutti will go there one day, though knowing him he'll hide himself away and no one will find where he is for thousands of years.

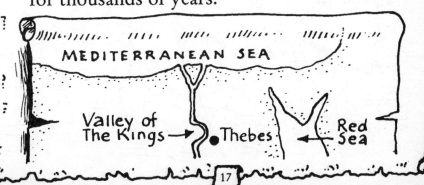

MEDITERRANEAN SEA

Valley of
The Kings → •Thebes ← Red Sea

I hope that if I visit there often enough I might find a nice place to go myself when the time comes to make my journey to the Underworld. Tutti's often saying he wishes I would stay in the Valley of Kings for good – he must think such a lot of me to have such a sweet idea.

Thousands of years ago pharaohs and other important people (like me) used to build great big pyramids for themselves. Pyramids are very grand, but they're not very comfortable. I wouldn't like to spend my afterlife inside one. I know I'd get lost and the idea of having all the stone piled up on top of me would give me the creeps. No, I'd be much happier in a nice cosy rock tomb, cut into the hillside, like the ones in the Valley of the Kings. It's a very nice neighbourhood too – a very good address when people come to see you.

Of course there's one tomb there we'd all love to move into. That's the fabulous temple built by a 'king' who must have been very much like me – anyway that's what I think.

This 'king' was actually a queen. Her name was Hatshepsut and she lived only 150 years ago. She showed them who was boss when she ruled Egypt! Oh, yes, they knew who gave the orders when Queen Hatshepsut was running the country. And her temple shows it. It's the first thing you see when you go to the Valley of the Kings. It's very grand. It would suit me very well. I must have a word with Tutti about it.

I'll take it!

5. Be a good mummy.

It must be having to leave Tutti for a long time that set me thinking about what it takes to be a mummy, and how I must be a *really* good mummy from now until I go away. I expect anyone can become a rotten mummy. To be a good mummy, one that people will still be talking about long after you've gone to the Underworld, that takes some doing. Naturally I want to be an extra-special mummy, so I looked up 'Mummies' in the Yellow Papyri and found this advertisement.

MUM'S THE WORD
BY APPOINTMENT TO THE PHARAOH

For all your Afterlife needs
Personal service guaranteed
Pay now – last for ever
Visit our
exclusive showroom on Karnak Way
'DON'T BE A DUMMY, BE OUR MUMMY'

With an invitation like that I was round at Karnak Way like an arrow from a bow. Mr Rappemtite, the head mummy man was very helpful. He showed me some lovely colour pictures painted on the wall and gave me their brochure which explains everything that has to be done if I'm going to be a good mummy.

It wasn't quite what I expected, but then so many things aren't quite what I expect.

Making The Most Of The Next Life

At MUM'S THE WORD we know how much we all enjoy life here on earth. That's why we want all our customers to get the best from the next life. And take Osiris's word for it, the next life is even better than this one!

MUM'S THE WORD has been sending customers onto the best of afterlives for centuries. With a good mummy that will last for ever you'll know your spirit will have somewhere safe and sound to rest for ever as well.

First we give you a good clean and take out the squidgy bits inside. (Don't worry, they're put into special jars to stay with you and we always make sure the heart goes back where it belongs.)

Next comes the drying stage. For forty days our customers are packed in a sort of salt – we call it natron in the trade. This soaks up all the moisture leaving you fresh and dry.

When that's over it's time for another wash and a rub with all your favourite spices to give you a heavenly smell your friends will envy until the day they die.

When you're quite ready we start the most skilful part of the process – the wrapping. Hundreds of metres of top-quality linen bandages are wrapped tightly round and round and round you. It takes two weeks from start to finish, but by the end you can be sure you'll stay in perfect shape for as long as you want.

We offer a choice of outer coverings ('coffins' in the trade). These range from the Lo-Kost to the gold-covered Pharaoh Special, but whichever you choose there'll be no mistaking whose mummy you are because we guarantee a life-like mask of you on the outside.

You can tell they offer a very good service. Lots of my old friends have been to them. They take care of everything. They send you off into the afterlife with all you could possibly need: furniture, food, boats to travel and fish in, clothes, games to play, statues to keep you company, musical instruments, chariots and hunting weapons, jewellery, even guide books to the Underworld – you name it, they'll make sure you have it. In fact they do such a good job that I have heard that dreadful robbers sometimes break in and steal things from you. If that's going to happen, I'd rather have everything out on show some-where, so that everyone can have a look at it. At least they'd see what a good mummy I am.

I must remember to tell Tutti about that.

Thebes - last day before my holiday

Thebes is such a nice city to live in. If I wasn't leaving for a fabulous luxury cruise I should be quite sorry to be going away. Of course I shall miss Tutti terribly and I am sure he won't know what to do with himself when I am away. That's why I wanted our last day together to be extra special and I made sure I was with him all day long – lucky boy.

He has to wake up very early every morning because there's always so much to do. Today, after I had rubbed noses with him to wish him good morning, I helped his servants wash and dress him, just like I did when he was a baby. Now he wears the proper clothes of a pharaoh and what a picture he looks in his little pleated skirt and royal head-dress.

He takes it all terribly seriously (bless him). The vizier arrived soon after he was dressed and gave a report on all the important things happening in the country. Couldn't he have waited until my little lamb had eaten his breakfast? I've never liked the vizier. He's too big for his boots if you ask me and I've told Tutti so.

'Mum,' he answered, 'I can't do it all by myself. I need other people to collect taxes, make the laws work, run the army, feed the people and keep the gods happy.'

Even so, I think he should start the day with a good breakfast.

It still seems strange to think of my little boy as a god. Since he became pharaoh, though, that's what he is and all the people think he's just as important as the rest of the gods. Every morning he has to go to the temple to say hello to the other gods and keep them on his side. Amun is the special god, that's why Tutti has his name at the end of his own – Tutankh*amun*. I felt so proud this morning when I watched him go into the temple to make an offering to the great god. I do hope he liked it. I wouldn't want Amun to be in a bad mood when I am sailing down the river.

After the temple, Tutti and I went to school. He pretended to be cross that I was going with him and stamped his foot and said only babies have their mummies with them in school. I think the poor lamb was trying to let the other children know just who was king. When he is older Tutti will have to spend most of the day running the country and greeting important visitors. At the moment he still has his lessons to do and it's every good parent's duty to help a child get on in life and answer all those tricky little questions that children try to catch them out with.

Watching Tutti sitting with the other

children listening to the scribe who was teaching them took me right back to when I was his age. The lessons were just as I remembered them. Now I understand what he means about school being boring and repetitive. I thought things might have changed, but they were exactly the same.

Even the stories they chanted aloud were the same as the ones I had to chant out loud at my school. There must be a better way of learning to read, but I suppose if there was we Egyptians would have discovered it. After all we are the best in the world at everything.

Tutti's lucky because he can practise writing on nice smooth sheets of papyrus. That's because he's the king. I did feel sorry for the others who have to make do with pieces of broken pottery or stone slates. Why is writing so difficult? Why can't we invent a machine that does the writing for us? Wouldn't that be marvellous? I had that idea as I watched them all struggling to draw the pictures that Inkyph Ums, the scribe, was teaching them.

I can remember when my scribe tried to teach me to write. First I had to chew the end of my reed pen until it was bushy like a paint brush. Then he made me mix my black ink and my red ink with water, just as you mix paint. Finally I had to copy the hieroglyphic pictures. I never did get the hang of them all and who can blame me? There are over 700 of them! I hope for Tutti's sake he can remember them better than I could.

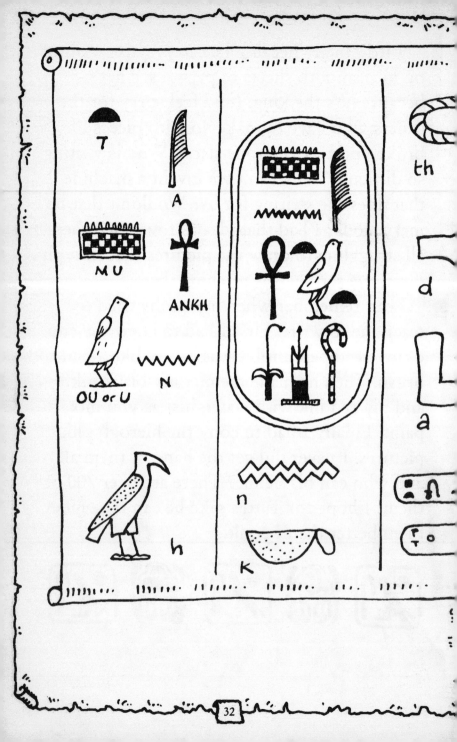

Reading wasn't much easier for me than writing, especially as the hieroglyphic picture thingies can be read in all sorts of different ways: left to right, tfel ot thgir (which is the other way round), or

v
e
r
t
i
c
a
l
l
y

it all depends which way the picture signs are facing.

Watching Tutti and his friends trying to copy what Inkyph Ums had given them, I wasn't surprised I had been confused. Inkyph Ums didn't have any patience with them. Just because he had learnt it all he still shouldn't have beaten their poor little backsides with his cane when they made mistakes. He was a real old bossy boots, but Tutti says all the scribes are the same. Because they can read and write without making mistakes they get all the top jobs and that makes them believe they're better than everybody else. Well, they're not better than Nefertipsy. . . Nefertyped. . . Nefertidly. . . Nefertiny. . . they're not better than me – because I'm the Pharaoh's mummy and don't let them forget it!

On the subject of forgetting things, I must remember to take my lumps of charcoal (to make black ink) and that hard red stuff called ochre (to make red ink). Come to think of it, where have I put the reed and palette for writing. . . Oh, silly me, I'm using them!

What would Tutti say?

After school it was home for tea, then I let
Tutti play with his toys before going to bed.
When I went to rub noses goodnight he was
sitting up in bed reading from that dreadful
book *The Curse of the Mummy's Tomb*. It
gives *me* the creeps just looking at it - why he
likes these horror stories, I'll never know. He
says all the other boys at school are reading
them too. Oh well, I suppose it's better than
not reading at all.

The Royal Barge
Day 1

Though it was very hard saying goodbye to dear little Tutti I've now started my cruise and I can see that this is the *only* way to travel. I know that most people in Egypt travel by boat. A few may have to walk to where they want to go and there are those dangerous chariots that some rich young men race about in, but no one except me can be travelling in style like this.

Most of our Egyptian boats have names that say something about them and this one certainly does. It's called *Tuttal Luxury* and that's exactly what it is. For one thing it's not made out of bundles of reeds like a lot of smaller, cheaper boats. Mine is built out of the most lovely smelling wood. This is called cedar and it has to be brought from the Byblos, a country round the coast from Egypt where the cedar trees grow to a great height. I have my own cabin which shades me from the sun as I lie on soft cushions and watch the river bank and other boats drifting past. There are servants to bring me food and drink, a little beer is my favourite when I'm thirsty. And there are lots of nice strong young men who row me along, led by the chief rower, Steferedgrafe, who wears a gold medal to show he's the best. Of course the royal barge has a sail, but I am

travelling northwards down the river. The
wind usually blows the other way, towards
the south. So we'll use the sail when we turn
round to come home back up the river.

Now I understand why the hieroglyphic
picture thingy meaning 'to travel south' has a

picture of a boat with a sail. The picture of a man with oars must mean 'to travel north'. I feel quite pleased with myself for working that out. Maybe that's why they say travel broadens the mind.

Day 5

After four days on board, we've stopped at Abydos which is a bit touristy because of Osiris. Tutti adores the story of Osiris and his sister Isis. I thought he'd cry when I told him about their wicked brother Seth who murdered Osiris and cut him into little pieces, but Tutti loved this bit. Especially when I got to the part of the story where Isis and the god Anubis collected all the bits of Osiris's body up and put him together again to rule the Underworld. Maybe that's why Tutti likes those horror stories he reads on his own now?

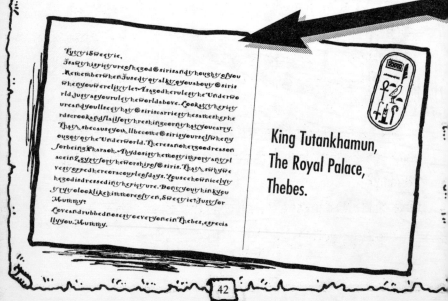

Tutti is sweetie,

Isn't this picture of the god Osiris and I thought of you. Remember when I used to talk to you about Osiris when you were little - I said he ruled the Underworld just as you ruled the world above. Look at the picture and you'll see that Osiris carried the same things the crooked staff and the threshing corn that you carry. That's because you'll become Osiris yourself when you set at the Underworld. There's another good reason for being Pharaoh. They deity the most important place in Egypt sort the worship of Osiris. That's why we very erred here a couple of days. You see how nicely the god is dressed in the picture. Don't you think you'll look like him more often, Sweetie? Just for Mummy?

Love and rubbed noses to everyone in Thebes, especially you. Mummy.

King Tutankhamun,
The Royal Palace,
Thebes.

Tutti Sweetie,

I saw this picture of the god Osiris and thought of you. Remember when I used to talk to you about Osiris when you were little? As a god he rules the Underworld, just as you rule the world above. Look at the picture and you'll see that Osiris carries the same shepherd's crook and flail for threshing corn that you carry. That's because you'll become Osiris yourself when you go to the Underworld. There's another good reason for being Pharaoh.

Abydos is the most important place in Egypt for the worship of Osiris. That's why we've stopped here for a couple of days.

You see how nicely the god is dressed in the picture. Don't you think you could try to look like him more often, Sweetie? Just for Mummy?

Love and rubbed noses to everyone in Thebes, especially you.

Mummy

The Royal Barge
Day 7

I've never been so ill before. Last night I felt as though I was being turned inside out. Nothing would stay down: beer, milk, bread, meat, fish – it was terrible. Luckily there was a very good doctor passing on his boat and he was brought to see me.

Now I've had my doubts about doctors in the past. They may be very good at mending broken bones and healing cuts, but with all the charms and potions they use to treat other things, they seem more like magicians sometimes. But this doctor, Sawboneandchopit, was obviously just the right one for an important patient like me. He asked what I had been eating and when I said I'd had some bread from the market he looked thoughtful and asked if there was any left for him to see.

One of the servants brought a piece, which he sniffed and tasted.

'The bread has made you ill, oh gracious one,' he told me, in such a nice way.

'But it was only baked yesterday,' I told him.

'Even so, the flour was not clean.' He explained that the baker in the market must have used flour from grain that is beaten on a floor covered in all sorts of awful animal dirt that I can't even begin to describe. Ugh! The doctor didn't seem the least surprised my tummy didn't like it. Apparently it's quite common. He told me I should be thankful that at home I eat bread from the royal bakery which is always beautifully clean. I think Tutti should pass a law to make all flour clean, otherwise his mummy will have an empty tummy for the rest of her holiday.

Tutti Sweetie,

I couldn't go by this dreadful place without sending a card to remind you how pleased Mummy is that you have gone back to the good old ways and the good old gods, unlike naughty Akhenaten when he was Pharaoh before you. The great god Amun must be very pleased as well. I can't imagine what Akhenaten was thinking of when he tried to make people stop worshipping Amun and start worshipping Aten instead. And as for leaving dear old Thebes to make a new capital at Akhetaten — well, he must have been barmy. But Mummy's clever boy put a stop to all that silly nonsense, didn't he? Now you're Pharaoh we're back in Thebes with the old gods and I don't expect naughty Akhenaten has joined them in the afterlife. He doesn't deserve to after the fuss he caused — serve him right.

Love and rubbed noses,

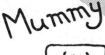

The Royal Barge

Day 10
Moored by the bank

I have just had a very embarrassing experience and the only one I can talk to about it is you, dear diary.

I feel so silly. The royal barge was brought in beside the bank so that the servants could go ashore to buy my lunch. While I was waiting for them to come back I saw a man on the bank working with a bucket on a long pole. On the other end of the pole was a weight. I was fascinated by what he was doing. First he swung the bucket out over the river and then dipped the pole, so that the bucket dropped in and filled with water. Then he pushed down on the weighted end of the pole. This raised the bucket back up to where the man was standing, so that he could catch hold of it and pour the water into a nearby ditch that ran into his fields. The work looked really quite easy. The weight on one end

makes the heavy bucket feel lighter when it's lifted and that must save so much hard work under the hot sun when the fields need to be given lots of water, so that the crops grow well.

I thought this looked so clever that I called over to him, 'What are you using?'

Now I may be getting a little deaf, but I'm sure I heard him answer 'Shove off' or 'Shut up' – whatever it was, it sounded very, very rude.

'What did you say?' I answered, crossly.

'Shove off,' he said again. I'm sure he did.

That's no way to talk to anyone in a boat as smart as mine and it's certainly no way to speak to the Pharaoh's mummy. So I warned him that if he didn't give me a proper answer my guards would arrest him.

But he kept on being rude until the soldiers grabbed him and dragged him across to the Captain of the Guard, who was about to cut him into little bits of crocodile lunch when the man spoke to him. The Captain of the Guard looked a bit awkward, put his sword away and came across to say, 'He's been trying to tell you the answer to your question, Your Majesty. It's a *shaduf*. That thing he's using is called a *shaduf*. That's what he's been saying all the time... Shall I let him go?'

What could I say? What will Tutti say when he finds out? I didn't know where to look. The worst thing was I had to give the man half my lunch as a way of saying sorry.

Dear Sweetie,

I saw this picture of a crocodile and thought of you. Isn't he looking at you? By the way it says at the bottom is that what you say about me?

There on the Royal Barge keep a lookout for crocodiles when we are close to the bank or are travelling along a canal leading from the river. I didn't realise how big they are or how fierce. They have huge teeth. I pointed them out to one of the crew who answered, "Silly, they are only crocodiles." He had a funny look in his eye when he said that. I rather hope a crocodile decided to suck in to him first.

Love and rubbed noses,
Mummy

King Tutankhamun,
The Royal Palace,
Thebes.

Tutti Sweetie,

I saw this picture of a crocodile and thought of you. Is it the look in its eyes? Or the way it snaps at people? Isn't that what you say about me?

The crew on the Royal Barge keep a look-out for crocodiles when we are close to the bank or are travelling along a canal leading from the river. I didn't realize how big they are, or how fierce. They have huge teeth. I pointed these out to one of the crew who answered, 'All the better to eat you with'. He had a funny look in his eye when he said that. I rather hope a crocodile decides to tuck into him first.

Love and rubbed noses,

Mummy

The Faiyum

Day 12

How lovely to have arrived at the Faiyum. Cruising in the Royal Barge is very comfortable, but it is wonderful to stretch my legs in this gorgeous house and garden.

Nicenkleen doesn't look a day older than when we were growing up together in the palace. Is her make-up a bit thicker, I wonder? She seems very pleased with her beautiful new house and who wouldn't be, with a husband as rich and successful as Munnyinthebank?

She has told me so much about living here and Tutti says it is one of the richest parts of the country so I am thrilled to be visiting the Faiyum for myself.

For once I have left the River Nile behind and come westwards, not into the awful Red Land, thank goodness, but to a huge rich, green, fertile place. Twink Eltwinkel, who gave me the map, says a place like this is called an oasis. All around is dry dusty desert, but here the land is lower and water comes to the surface to make a huge lake. I think it's heavenly.

Munnyinthebank owns a large estate with masses of peasants and slaves who farm the land. From my room I can see fields of corn, herds of cattle and goats and pigs, ponds full of fish and trees full of dates. I shan't go hungry here, but I must have a quiet word with Nicenkleen about the bread. After what the doctor told me about dirty flour I can't be too careful.

The Faiyum

Day 13

Munnyinthebank gave me a very interesting day out today. I had thought I might sit around the house chatting to Nicenkleen, eating dates and trying a wine drink they make from grapes. But he insisted on showing me all round his estate, in the hot sunshine. How kind.

He took me to see the fields where the corn grows. I know that bread comes from flour but I'd always been a bit puzzled where the flour comes from. The answer is stuff called corn. The peasants make their bread from a sort of corn called barley. I wouldn't recommend eating that. The bread we eat is much nicer. That is made from wheat.

Anyhow, the corn is sown in the fields when the Nile mud has covered them after the flooding, which starts at New Year. That time of flood is the first season of the year. A sweet little peasant told me that – as if I didn't already

know! The next season is the busy time of planting and growing. First the peasants have to plough the soil with their wooden ploughs. Some use cattle to pull them, but I've seen others pulling the ploughs themselves. Talk about hot, sweaty work. I don't know how many times they need to change. Come to think of it they wear so little perhaps they don't change their clothes at all. Phew!

When the seed is on the ground, herds of animals trample over the fields to press it in. After this there's still a long way to go until the bread. As the corn grows, the peasants have to dig out the weeds and water the fields until the third and final season of the year.

This is the hot dry one when the corn ripens and the peasants harvest it, cutting the corn with their wooden sickles fitted with sharp teeth made of flint. The way Munnyinthebank described it, it all sounded so easy. What a pity they can't always keep the grain clean when they thresh it on the floor. Not to mention the grit that gets in with the flour as well. I'm sure chewing gritty bread is wearing my teeth away. When I look at them in my copper mirror, they don't look the same as they used to.

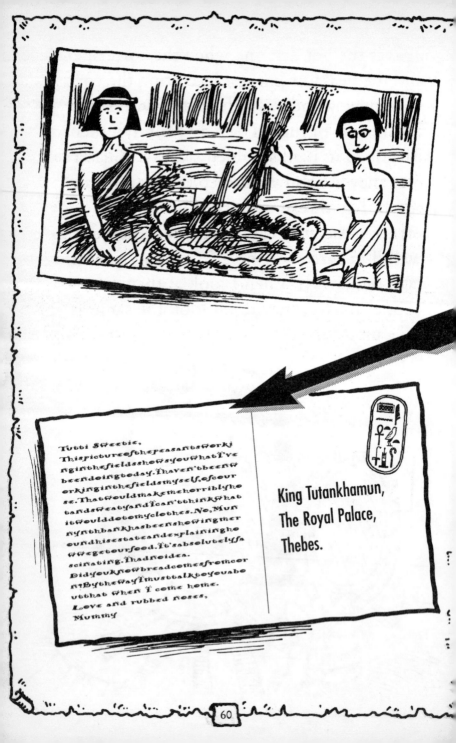

Tutti Sweetie,

This picture of the peasants working in the fields shows you what I've been doing today. I haven't been working in the fields myself, of course. That would make me horribly hot and sweaty and I can't think what it would do to my clothes. No, Mummy Nynthban Kha has been showing me around his estate and explaining how we get our food. It's absolutely fascinating. I had no idea.

Did you know bread comes from corn? By the way I must talk to you about that when I come home.

Love and rubbed noses,

Mummy

King Tutankhamun,
The Royal Palace,
Thebes.

Tutti Sweetie,

This picture of the peasants working in the fields shows you what I've been doing today. I haven't been working in the fields myself, of course. That would make me horribly hot and sweaty and I can't think what it would do to my clothes. No, Munnyinthebank has been showing me round his estate and explaining how we get our food. It's absolutely fascinating. I had no idea.

Did you know bread comes from corn? By the way I must talk to you about that when I come home.

Love and rubbed noses,

Mummy

The Faiyum
Day 14

After the exhausting day in the fields with Munnyinthebank I was so pleased to have a nice lazy day at home with Nicenkleen.

This new house, new villa I suppose I should call it really, would suit me very well. It's so bright and clean you'd never know it's built entirely of mud bricks. Even the floors and ceilings are made of mud. But everything's covered in paint so you'd never guess.

All round the outside of the garden is a tall white wall. Inside there are trees growing tasty things like dates and figs, and a pool full of juicy fat fish. It's nice to sit here in the shade to enjoy the cool of the day. The roof is flat of course, at least we don't have to worry about rain in Egypt! So we can sit up there at night as well.

Nicenkleen has her own part of the house, where the children and other women in the house live too. That's where I'm staying. Munnyinthebank has his own rooms where he does his business and there are some wonderful big rooms where they have parties and entertain people. I suppose the servants and slaves live somewhere in the outbuildings. I don't think I want to go and find out.

All the rooms are beautifully cool, in spite of the heat outside. I suppose only having little windows high up in the walls must help. They let in all the light you need, but keep out the hot sun.

What I really like is the furniture. There isn't much, people like us don't like to be cluttered with lots of furniture – we enjoy the space. But the furniture they do have must be very expensive. The beds have got leather straps which make them very comfortable. I expect I will soon get used to the wooden headrest they've given me as a pillow. The chairs have leather straps too and they are beautifully decorated with carved painted wood, and inlaid with precious metal. I can't imagine how much money they must have spent.

Some of the walls are painted with nice pictures, others have expensive wall-hangings. There's even a special little room where I can go when I 'need to go' and a servant cleans out the 'need to go' hole in the floor every day so it's never unpleasant in there, which is nice to know.

On the north side of the house, and I know it's north because Twink Eltwinkel explained that to me, they've built a shady veranda which catches the cool evening breezes. That's where Nicenkleen and I played a game of senet today. I concentrated really hard on moving my counters round the grid, trying to overcome the obstacles and reach Osiris but I never seem to win board games like senet. Is it because everyone else cheats? Surely my oldest friend wouldn't do that? Would she?

King Tutankhamun,
The Royal Palace,
Thebes.

Tutti Sweetie,

You must try the wine they make here. I am bringing jars of it home with me and I know you will enjoy it. It's quite sweet, which you like. But I think it's even better mixed with honey. You need to be careful how much you drink, though. I think I may have been a bit silly when I tried some for the first time.

Munnyinthebank took me and Nicenkleen to the place where they make it and gave us some to drink while the peasants crushed the grapes with their feet in a big square trough, so that the juice can run out.

Maybe it was the hot sun, but after the peasants had finished pressing the grapes and I had finished quite a few cups of wine, I felt so happy I decided I wanted to have a go in the trough myself. Before anyone could stop me, I had climbed in over the side and was squelching in the grapes almost up to my knees. I must say I was doing just as well as the peasants, only they had been holding ropes hanging above the trough to stay steady and I couldn't reach these. I was so happy though, it didn't seem to matter — until I must have slipped and fallen over.

Nicenkleen was very understanding when they hauled me out. She says the grape juice colour quite suits my dress. I'm not so sure. In fact I suddenly don't feel very well. I think I had better lie down, Sweetie. Love and rubbed noses,

Mummy

The Faiyum
Day 17

I've had a very good rest here, but I shall be happy to get back to the Nile again and carry on down river.

Tonight Nicenkleen has told the cook to give us my favourite things for supper, so I can't wait to sit down and be brought all sorts of delicious dishes by the serving girls. This is the menu that is being prepared in my honour:

ROAST GOOSE
BOILED BEEF
GRILLED FISH
ONIONS
GARLIC ← *lots of it*
LEEKS
SWEET PASTRY WITH HONEY
yummy → DATES
POMEGRANATES
FIGS
GRAPES

poo!

I expect Munnyinthebank will give us some of his best wine too. I wonder if I should stick to the beer after what happened the last time I drank the wine? I know what Tutti would want me to do. But I am on holiday, so why shouldn't I enjoy myself? Wine it is!

The Royal Barge
Days 18 to 22 (I think)

The last few days seem to have gone by in a bit of a haze and I'm sorry, dear diary, that I haven't written you up for quite a while. It must have been that last night at The Faiyum. I remember deciding to enjoy myself and taking the odd sip of wine, but I don't remember much about being carried on to the Royal Barge or anything else.

Next stop Memphis and some *serious* shopping.

Memphis

After staying in Nicenkleen's fabulous new villa I didn't think anywhere could beat it. But this house in Memphis belonging to my old friends Helvis and Presletitti is almost as big and expensive as Tutti's palace. As the old capital of Egypt, Memphis is where the King used to live, and there are lots of big houses in the city, but this must be one of the grandest.

Yesterday evening they gave a huge feast to celebrate my arrival. Helvis is a very important official in Tutti's government. He is very rich and powerful and lots of his rich and powerful friends came to share the feast. I haven't had such a good time for ages.

I was able to wear my newest dress, the one I bought specially for grand feasts like this. It's in the very latest style, all white and made of the thinnest linen you can buy. There's a very flattering tunic that goes on first and over this is a full-length gown of lovely pleated material that hangs from my shoulders right down to my ankles. As this was an extra-special occasion, I also put on a net of red and blue beads across my tunic. It may be a bit difficult to sit down with this on, but it looks stunning and everyone was admiring my outfit. Tutti would have felt so proud – at least I hope he would.

The other great success of the night was my new wig. I have different wigs to wear for different occasions – as the Pharaoh's mummy I have to look my best all the time. This feasting wig is quite long and has several layers of curls that fall over my left shoulder. I think it makes me look like a girl again, though I thought I heard one of the silly young women giggling to her friend and asking, as she pointed to me, 'Who's that old dear wearing the black sheepskin on her head?' I must have been mistaken – this wig is decorated with some of my nicest jewels. It's the height of fashion – at least that's what the wig-maker told me.

It took most of the afternoon to get ready for the feast. In my position you can't leave anything to chance. After rubbing myself all over with oil and perfume, it was time for my make-up. As a leader of Egyptian fashion I use black powder called kohl to put a darker border round my eyes and blacken my eyebrows. Blue eyeshadow suits me best, though some of the others looked very striking with green eyeshadow. Red ochre powder gives colour to my cheeks and I use a red ointment to make my lips look just right. Only when I'm completely happy with the way I look in the mirror, do I let my servant put the wig on my head.

Then it's time to put the scented cone on top of my wig and go into the feast. The scented cone is a super idea. When a lot of people get together in hot places, even posh people like the ones Helvis and Preslettiti invited, there's always a chance the air could start to pong after a while. So we put these perfumed cones on our heads and during the evening they slowly melt and let sweet-smelling oil run down all over us. That way everyone smells nice all evening.

I always feel sorry for the servants and the dancing girls. It must be so hot for them, they wear practically nothing. Many of the men feel sorry for the dancing girls too. I notice that they keep staring at them. At least they don't feel sorry for me in that way.

Of course the servants were busy all evening bringing us dishes of food and jars of wine and beer. I don't think twice about eating with my fingers in company like this. I'm sure everyone at this feast always washes their hands before they touch food.

I had a very nice time chatting to the women, finding out about Memphis. The men sit in a separate group so I don't know what they were talking about, but I like to think I heard my name mentioned once or twice. One of them told what must have been a joke. He said he'd heard that Tutti had sent me on this cruise hoping that I'd be gobbled up by a crocodile or a hippopotamus. All the other men laughed. Apart from that it was a very nice evening and I was very good about the wine.

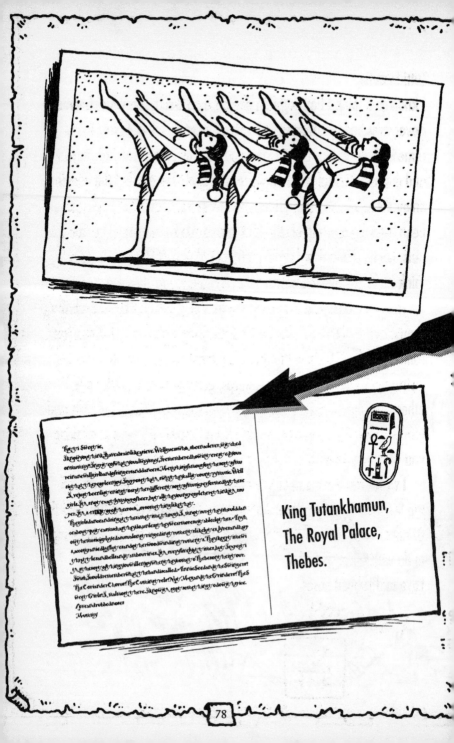

King Tutankhamun,
The Royal Palace,
Thebes.

Tutti Sweetie,

I know you think I have a brain like a sieve. Well guess who's been a clever, switched-on mummy? In spite of what you always say, I remembered how interested you are in a new all-girl band of singers and dancers. Memphis is famous for the sort of music that the people enjoy. I suppose that's why they call it country music. Well, I've just been listening to a rather different sort of music performed by these girls. It's not exactly my cup of beer, but all the young people here think it's super. It's 'top of the crocs', or something like that.

The girls dance and sing at the same time, though I'm not sure they should dance about quite as much as they do, unless they wear more suitable clothes. Anyhow the music is played as usual on stringed instruments like lutes, lyres and harps, accompanied by flutes and other woodwind instruments. They keep time with rattles and bells and tambourines. It's very lively at times, but I expect it's the sort of thing you will enjoy when they come to Thebes on their tour.

I wish I could remember what the band is called. Annie Seed and the Swingers? The Coriander Chorus? The Cuminstrels? Nut Meg and the Grinders? The Sweet Girls? I'm almost there. I know it's got something to do with spice.

Love and rubbed noses

Mummy

Memphis

Day 25

I don't like sightseeing at the best of times – and today definitely wasn't the best of times.

I'm sure Helvis meant well when he suggested I might enjoy spending a day all by myself right away from his house, but I can't believe he had a day like this in mind.

I suppose everyone who comes to Memphis has to look round where the great King used to live. His name was Narmer and he made himself the first Pharaoh hundreds and hundreds of years ago. Until Narmer took charge, Egypt was divided into two kingdoms, Upper Egypt, which is down in the south and Lower Egypt, closer to the delta at the other end of the Nile, where it flows into the sea. Narmer took the crowns of both kingdoms and made them into one crown which all the pharaohs have worn ever since, right down to Tutti. Memphis is on the boundary between Upper and Lower Egypt.

That's why Narmer built his capital here and that's why Helvis sent me off to see the sites.

If I had been given a map, I'm sure I wouldn't have had any trouble finding my way about. As it was, I must have got slightly lost. It's easy to do. Once you leave the main streets, the lanes between the houses are very narrow (and very smelly) and they all look the same. I'm sure even clever Twink Eltwinkel would get lost without a map.

For one thing all the houses are the same colour, mud brown from the mud bricks. They look identical – little square boxes with flat roofs reached by a staircase. I went inside one and asked the lady who lived there if I could go up onto her roof to see where I was. But when I got up on top all I could see were lots and lots of other flat roofs and the river away in the distance.

The lady in the house was quite helpful and tried to give me directions. I thought I was being helpful too. She was making bread and I didn't think the flour she was using looked terribly nice. So I told her she ought to get some clean flour that didn't have animal nasties and dirt in it.

I'm sorry she didn't like what I said. She told me to get lost, which didn't help, because if I hadn't been lost I wouldn't have gone to see her in the first place.

It took me hours to find my way out of that maze of little alleys. I stumbled into a dark little workshop where a potter was making a pot on a sort of wheel thing he was moving with his hand. Coming from the bright sunlight I couldn't see where I was going. Even so I don't think he should have shouted so rudely when I knocked over the three other pots he had just made.

I had an even closer shave in another poky little workshop. It was terribly hot and I could see a lot of smoke. The men inside had almost no clothes on and were running with sweat. I tried to ask directions but they shouted that if I didn't move I'd be a copper statue. I didn't understand what they meant until I saw two of them lifting a big basin full of runny copper off a glowing furnace. Apparently I was standing in front of the moulds they were going to pour it into. I didn't stay to watch how they got on.

Tutti Sweetie

When I was shopping today this dear man was so excited that the Pharaoh's mummy had been to his shop that he insisted on giving me his card and asking me to send it to you. I bought a pair of his sandals which make my feet sore, so I don't think I'll be buying any more, but he does seem awfully clever at making all sorts of things out of bundles of old reeds. If there's anything you'd like as a present? Let me know and I'll stop off on the way back home.

Love and rubbed noses,

Mummy

Papyrus Pepi

PERFECT PAPYRUS PRODUCTS OUR SPECIALITY

YOU NAME IT, WE MAKE IT – AND ALL FROM

PAPYRUS:

BASKETS
BOATS
BOXES
BRUSHES

NETS
PAPER
ROPE
SANDALS

AND PLENTY, PLENTY MORE

I saw a lot of people working that afternoon in their cramped little houses: carpenters sawing wood with copper saws and shaping it with copper chisels; men making ropes from leather; weavers making cloth – but none of them told me where I wanted to go. If I hadn't been so exhausted I would have liked to stay and watch the jeweller I saw drilling holes in lovely coloured beads to string them on a necklace.

WE ALL HAD A 'SMASHING' TIME!

He was using a very fine drill around which he'd wrapped a bowstring that was attached to a bow. When he pulled this quickly backwards and forwards, the drill whizzed round and made a hole in the bead. The carpenters I saw were using bigger ones just like it for drilling holes in wood.

I'd almost given up ever finding my way back to Helvis's house when I spotted a man I thought I'd seen visiting Preslettiti. He was a glass worker and because things made of glass are only for rich, important people like Helvis, Preslettiti and me, I was sure he could tell me how to find my way back to their house.

In fact he was very kind and took me all the way back himself. I was so grateful to him that I felt I had to buy something he'd made to say thank you. A glass hippopotamus may not have been my first choice, but he said Tutti would like it very much. I hope he does and I hope it doesn't get broken on the way home because it was very, very expensive.

King Tutankhamun,
The Royal Palace,
Thebes.

TAKE A SPIN IN THE NEW SUPER-
POWERED, TWIN-HORSE PHARRARHI
AND LEAVE EVERYONE BEHIND
EATING YOUR DUST! CHOOSE YOUR
OWN POWER-PACK FROM OUR TOP-
OF-THE-RANGE STABLES. ALL HORSES
COME IN MATCHING COLOURS.
THEY RUN ON EASY-TO-FIND HAY
AND WATER. THEY'LL PUT YOU
ALONGSIDE ANY GAZELLE YOU
HUNT AND RUN DOWN ANY
ENEMY STUPID ENOUGH TO
FIGHT YOU. STYLISH, SLEEK AND
HARD OVER THE GROUND
(SPRINGS ARE FOR WIMPS), THE
NEW PHARRARHI CHAR...

Tutti Sweetie,
I know how much you enjoy racing about in
sports chariots and even though I think they
are awful things, I thought you would like to
see the latest model they're driving around in
here.
Sometimes I wish the wheel had never been
invented. You'd have thought they could have
found something more useful to do with it
than fix two of them to a silly little basket
thing and tie it to the back of two horses. You
may say I make a fuss, but the way some young
men drive them, they ought to be locked up in
prison. Maybe I'm just old-fashioned, but I
don't see why people can't travel by boat if
they want to go somewhere. I know you can't
hunt desert animals with bows and arrows
and fight land battles from a boat, but it's
much more comfortable – and much safer.
Love and rubbed noses,
Mummy

Tutti Sweetie,

I know how much you enjoy racing about in sports chariots and even though I think they are awful things, I thought you would like to see the latest model they're driving around in here.

Sometimes I wish the wheel had never been invented. You'd have thought they could have found something more useful to do with it than fix two of them to a silly little basket thing and tie it to the back of two horses. You may say I make a fuss, but the way some young men drive them, they ought to be locked up in prison. Maybe I'm just old-fashioned, but I don't see why people can't travel by boat if they want to go somewhere. I know you can't hunt desert animals with bows and arrows and fight land battles from a boat, but it's much more comfortable — and much safer.

Love and rubbed noses,

Mummy

TAKE A SPIN IN THE NEW SUPER-POWERED, TWIN-HORSE PHARRARHI AND LEAVE EVERYONE BEHIND EATING YOUR DUST! CHOOSE YOUR OWN POWER-PACK FROM OUR TOP-OF-THE-RANGE STABLES. ALL HORSES COME IN MATCHING COLOURS. THEY RUN ON EASY-TO-FIND HAY AND WATER. THEY'LL PUT YOU ALONGSIDE ANY GAZELLE YOU HUNT AND RUN DOWN ANY ENEMY STUPID ENOUGH TO FIGHT YOU. STYLISH, SLEEK AND HARD OVER THE GROUND (SPRINGS ARE FOR WIMPS), THE NEW PHARRARHI CHARIOT WILL MAKE YOU KING OF THE ROAD FROM THEBES TO MEMPHIS. REMEMBER OUR MOTTO -

'YOU'LL SMILE BESIDE THE NILE IN A CHARIOT FROM PHARRARHI.'

HIPPOPOTAMUS ON THE NILE

King Tutankhamun,
The Royal Palace,
Thebes.

Tutti Sweetie,

No prizes for saying what this huge animal is. (Just between ourselves I got a little muddled and said it was an elephant, but the man in the postcard shop told me very nicely that it wasn't an elephant. An elephant has a trunk and big ears. As you can see a hippopotamus doesn't have a trunk and only has tiny ears. Otherwise they look very similar. Don't they?)

Do you know how much damage a hippo can do when it gets into the fields? I have seen hunters out looking for hippos to stop them destroying the crops. It looks awfully dangerous. The boats they use are only small and they have to try to get the hippo tangled in ropes before they spear it with long spears and drag it to the bank.

I wonder what hippo steak tastes like? It would certainly be very big. Perhaps we should try one when I get home?

Love and rubbed noses,

Mummy

Day 30

We've arrived at Giza at last and it's very, very HOT.

I suppose the pyramids here are quite impressive, but it seems an awful lot of hard work for an awful lot of people just to build a big pile of stones. Apparently the Great Pyramid that King Cheops built 1200 years ago is the biggest stone building anywhere in the world. I expect it always will be the biggest. Most people have got better things to do with their time.

Still Tutti has paid for me to come all the way here to see the pyramids at Giza, so I had better show some interest. The guide who showed me round was very enthusiastic. I wish I could remember half the things he said.

Looking at the pyramid from the outside the sides are smooth and shiny. That's because they are covered with very smooth limestone which the builders polished to make it shine in the sun. The top stone was covered in gold when it was first built – just think of it. The guide made me take a close look and I must admit they all fitted perfectly. I don't think I could have fitted a sheet of writing papyrus into the gaps between the big stones. Though it won't surprise me if some naughty people don't come along and pinch these nice smooth stones to build something new for themselves.

THE BIGGEST PYRAMID IN THE WORLD – PROBABLY

Underneath these smooth casing stones there are layers and layers of big blocks of stone. The guide says these weigh over two tonnes each and every one has been carefully cut and shaped, so that it makes a perfect fit alongside the others.

All the stone comes from quarries on the eastern side of the Nile, where the cities are. The pyramids are on the western side, the side where the sun dies at the end of the day. It's to the west that the pharaohs travel when they go to the afterlife, so it's on the west of the river that they begin their journey to the Underworld.

The blocks have to be brought across on boats. That's easy though, compared with the very strong granite blocks that are used in some places inside the pyramid. They have to come down the river all the way from Aswan which is even further up the river than Thebes. What a journey with a great weight like that on board! I do think some of these old pharaohs were selfish.

To pile the blocks on top of each other, the guide says that gangs of men pulled them up sloping ramps on wooden sledges. There must have been hundreds of blocks on the move at the same time and thousands of men working on the building. Even so I must admit they did it very well. As far as I can see the pyramids at Giza are all perfectly shaped from top to bottom and all four sides look just the same.

The guide says they are supposed to look like the rays of sun falling on the earth. I got quite confused looking at them and trying to remember which direction I was facing. I still think Tutti is better off with his nice rock tomb and I shall tell him that when I get home. Old Cheops was a bit of a show-off if you ask me, though I didn't tell the guide that. I don't think he would have stopped talking if I had and I was worn out from walking round and round the three pyramids listening to him rambling on. I shall be glad to get back to the Royal Barge to cool down and write some more postcards to Tutti.

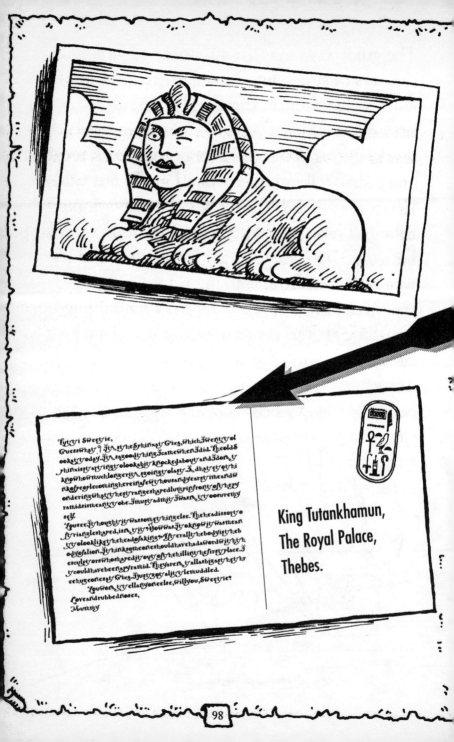

King Tutankhamun,
The Royal Palace,
Thebes.

Tutti Sweetie,

Guess what! It's the Sphinx at Giza, which I went to look at today. It's a good thing I came when I did. The old Sphinx is starting to look a bit knocked about and I don't know how much longer it's going to last. I'd hate to think of people coming here in a few thousand years time and wondering what the strange shaped lump in front of the pyramids is meant to be. I must admit I wasn't too sure myself.

You see I thought it was something else. The head is sort of triangle-shaped, isn't it? How was I to know it was meant to look like the head of a king? After all the body is the body of a lion. I think someone should have had a word with the sculptors who shaped it out of the hill in the first place. It could have been a pyramid. They aren't all as big as the three huge ones at Giza. I just got a little muddled.

You won't tell anyone else, will you, Sweetie?

Love and rubbed noses,

Mummy

A HUNTING CAT

Littyl Sweetie,

Jem, tyhisadearlittylekittyycaty. Jsawonejustylikeittyo day whenwe grasseed so the noutyhuntyinginythemarshesof the Delta, whichiswherewecarenow, bytheway.

The River Nile dividesintyoseveralchannelshereasitysflows slowlytowardytethesea, sotyhereisalotyofsrichlandyforsarthi ngandalotyofmarshesforhuntying.

Thehuntyerswecanwerecatyerbirdstyhatyliveinythereedb eds. Thecatyswereusedtyofrishtyentythebirdsintytytheair, s otyhatytheuntyerscouldtythrowtytheirspecialhuntyingstyi ckatyohittytyhem. Jtylookedalmostyasdifficultyasshootyinga runningaxcellewityhabowandarrowsfromtytheartfulchario tyofyours. Jsupposejtyscallameryteryofractyice.

Loveandrubbednoses,

Mumthy

King Tutankhamun,
The Royal Palace,
Thebes.

Tutti Sweetie,

Isn't this a dear little kitty cat? I saw one just like it today when we passed some men out hunting in the marshes of the Delta, which is where we are now, by the way.

The River Nile divides into several channels here as it flows slowly towards the sea, so there is a lot of rich land for farming and a lot of marshes for hunting.

The hunters we saw were after birds that live in the reed beds. The cats were used to frighten the birds into the air, so that the hunters could throw their special hunting sticks to hit them. It looked almost as difficult as shooting a running gazelle with a bow and arrow from that awful chariot of yours. I suppose it's all a matter of practise.

Love and rubbed noses,

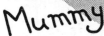

Heliopolis
Day 32

If I see one more tourist site I think I shall eat my wig. It was very kind of Tutti to give me this holiday, but I'm quite ready to go home now and this is the place where we turn round, hoist the sail and make our way back up the Nile to Thebes. We should be home for New Year, hooray!

This afternoon I've been brought to look at a great tall piece of carved rock which the people are terribly proud of. It's been standing here for a little over a hundred years and all four sides are covered with hieroglyphic picture thingies which I can't read very well. The top of this tall stone thing is pointed and from a distance it looks more like a great big needle to me than an obelisk –

I think that's what the guide called it.

I do find it confusing trying to keep track of which of the gods is being praised on this thing, and everything else that's dedicated to the gods. There are so many gods, that's the trouble.

I don't include Amun of course. He is the creator god who looks after Tutti and the whole country. But the others get me into a right old muddle, especially as so many of them have human bodies but animal heads.

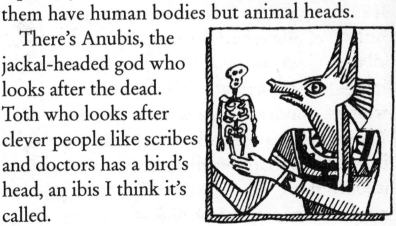

There's Anubis, the jackal-headed god who looks after the dead. Toth who looks after clever people like scribes and doctors has a bird's head, an ibis I think it's called.

Then there's Khnum who has the head of a ram, he looks after the rough parts of the river Nile called the cataracts – Khnum tells Hapy when it's time to make the Nile flood.

Hathor, the goddess of love, has the ears and horns of a cow – I can think of several

ladies who've said nasty things about me who look like cows and still see themselves as love goddesses.

And so it goes on. Sometimes I'm not sure which god I am supposed to be thanking or making an offering to. I hope they don't mind too much.

I don't even know which gods this stone obelisk thing was made for. The only good thing about it is that I can lean against it while

I write this page.

If only the sun wasn't so hot. It makes me feel so drowsy... so sleepy... I think I might close my eyes for a moment... I'll dream of somewhere nice and cool, somewhere far away where the sky is cloudy and it's cold and wet... so sleepy... I must make sure I don't let you, dear diary, and all Tutti's postcards slip down any of the gaps around the bottom of the ob... obeli... the object I'm sitting against. That would be too awful...

I must put down my ink and writing reed before I fall... before I fall fast... Before I fall fast aslee...

PUBLISHER'S ADDENDUM

Although the descriptions of life in Ancient Egypt and the facts contained in this diary are accurate, there is no historical evidence that King Tutankhamun had a mummy called Nefertidy and certainly by the time his 'mummy' was found, he was not alive. Nor does it seem likely that there were ever people living in Ancient Egypt with names like Ankhy Pankhy, Twink Eltwinkel, Nicencleen, Helvis and Preslettiti.

It seems obvious to us that Clive Dickinson has been had – he's dug up a hoax. Whoever sold him the lunch box spun a good story. So did the two so-called 'Egyptian experts' of whom we can find no trace. We only hope that Mr Dickinson did not pay too much for the lunch box and its phoney contents.

Cleopatra's Needle is genuine, of course, and can be seen standing beside the River Thames in London, but the story about the 'discovery' underneath it now seems very unlikely in the light of other evidence of forgery

As publishers we can only apologise and advise our readers not to believe every story they are told when they set out to look for a bargain.

THE REAL TUTANKHAMUN

Tutankhamun ruled Egypt as a boy pharoah more than 3300 years ago. He became pharoah when he was about nine years old in around 1345 BC and he died eight or nine years later. He was survived by his wife and childhood friend Ankhesenpaton and many drawings show that the royal couple grew up to be happily married teenagers.

Although Tutankhamun's reign lasted less than ten years and he was still young when he died, historians know far more about his life and reign than they do about many other Egyptian pharoahs because of the discovery of his tomb in 1922. Unlike the burial places of many pharoahs, his tomb had not been seriously damaged by robbers. Howard Carter, the archaeologist who made the discovery, found the young pharoah's final resting place filled with almost all the objects that had been left with him when he set out on his journey to the Underworld. Among the furniture, clothes, jewels and everyday objects, Carter found a tiny wreath of flowers – possibly the last farewell offering of the girl queen. But his most spectacular find was the young pharoah's mummy complete with its famous gold death mask. This is the only 'mummy' of Tutankhamun's about which anyone can be certain, but it is one of the most famous ever to have been found from the days of Ancient Egypt.

THE LOST DIARY OF ERIK BLOODAXE, VIKING WARRIOR

VIKING SCANDAL – GORBLIME TELLS ALL!

Newly discovered diaries and logbook cuttings reveal that famous Viking king, Erik Bloodaxe, couldn't write. However, his court poet Gorblime could and he gives astonishing details of life in Viking times.

- Battles and butchery
- Longships and love
- Births, marriages and plenty of deaths
- Poems and prisoners
- Erik's victories and his wife's vengeance
- Viking gods and Viking myths
- Travel and addventure

and much, much more.

THE LOST DIARY OF JULIUS CAESAR'S SLAVE

ROMAN SCANDAL – SLAVE TELLS ALL!

Newly discovered diaries (and bloodstained togas) reveal that Julius Caesar was careless! His slave, Commonus Muccus - a surprisingly educated man - reveals astonishing details about life in Ancient Roman times.

- Triumphs and togas
- Soldiers and slaves
- Centurions and Cleopatra
- Friends, Romans and countrymen
- Bards and barbarians
- Gods and Gladiators
- Roman sleaze and politics
- All the fun of the Circus Maximus
- And much, much more!

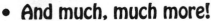

Order Form

To order direct from the publishers, just make a list of the titles you want and fill in the form below:

Name ....

Address ....

....

....

Send to: Dept 6, HarperCollins Publishers Ltd, Westerhill Road, Bishopbriggs, Glasgow G64 2QT.

Please enclose a cheque or postal order to the value of the cover price, plus:

UK & BFPO: Add £1.00 for the first book, and 25p per copy for each additional book ordered.

Overseas and Eire: Add £2.95 service charge. Books will be sent by surface mail but quotes for airmail despatch will be given on request.

A 24-hour telephone ordering service is available to holders of Visa, MasterCard, Amex or Switch cards on 0141- 772 2281.

Collins
An *Imprint* of HarperCollins*Publishers*